Cliffo

The Big Red Detective

Adapted by Gail Herman from the television script
"The Doggy Detectives" by Larry Swerdlove
Illustrated by Robbin Cuddy

Based on the Scholastic book series
"Clifford The Big Red Dog"
by Norman Bridwell

SCHOLASTIC INC.

New York Toronto London Auckland Sydney
Mexico City New Delhi Hong Kong Buenos Aires

ISBN 0-439-47315-2

10 9 8 7 6 5 4 3 2 1 03 04 05 06 07

Printed in the U.S.A.
First printing, February 2003

Contents

Let's Play!

Clifford The Big Red Dog was playing in his backyard. He smiled down at his friends. Then he wagged his tail. Back and forth. Back and forth. Just like a fan. Wind blew. Trees shook.

"Easy does it." Cleo's poodle fur stood on end.

"Sorry, Cleo." Clifford stopped. "It's such a nice day! I just felt like wagging."

“Yeah,” said T-Bone. The bulldog grinned. “I know that feeling. What should we do today?”

The dogs and their families lived on Birdwell Island. Clifford loved being here with his owner, Emily Elizabeth, her parents, and all the other dogs. The island had lots of open spaces. It was perfect for dogs — especially a big one like Clifford.

“We can play hide-and-seek in the woods,” said Clifford.

"Or swim at the beach," T-Bone said.

"Or run around the playground," Cleo added.

"We can do it all!" said Clifford. "But first, let's get K.C.! He loves all that stuff!"

K.C. was another dog friend. He had only three legs. But that didn't stop him from doing most things his friends could do.

A Good Story

Right that very minute, K.C. wasn't running or swimming or playing. He was sitting quietly on the porch.

K.C. tipped his head, listening to his owner.

Mrs. Young read out loud from a book:

" 'Hey, Schultzy,' said Detective Mike. 'Looks like I finally got you.' "

K.C. leaned closer. He knew Schultzy was the bad guy. And Detective Mike was the good guy.

" 'Yeah.' Schultzy sighed. 'You are too smart for me, Detective Mike.' "

Mrs. Young held the book open. "See?" she told K.C. "That's Schultzy. And that's the end of the book."

K.C. looked at the picture. He wagged his

tail. Mrs. Young yawned and closed the book.

"Yip!" K.C. nosed the book. He wanted more.

Mrs. Young shook her head. "I know you like that book, K.C. We'll take it back to the library and get another Detective Mike story tomorrow. Right now, though, I'm going to rest. You can play with your friends."

"Yip!" K.C. licked her face. Then he ran down the steps.

"Oops!" He plowed right into Clifford. Gently, Clifford lifted him up. Now they could see eye to eye.

"Hi, K.C. We were coming to get you. Want to play?"

"Sure!" said K.C. "Hi, Cleo! Hi, T!"

"Hi!" Cleo wagged her tail. "Let's go to the playground!"

"Last one there is a rotten dog biscuit!" said Clifford.

Minutes later, the dogs raced into the playground.

Screech! Clifford dug his giant paws into the ground. Dirt and sand flew everywhere. Cleo and K.C. came next, running through the dust.

Cleo turned to look for T-Bone. "Ha!" She laughed. "Looks like you're last, T. You're the dog biscuit!"

T-Bone rushed past. "Maybe. But I'm going to be the first one on the merry-go-round!"

He jumped into the air. "Whooaaa!" he said. There was nothing underneath him! He landed in the dirt with a thud.

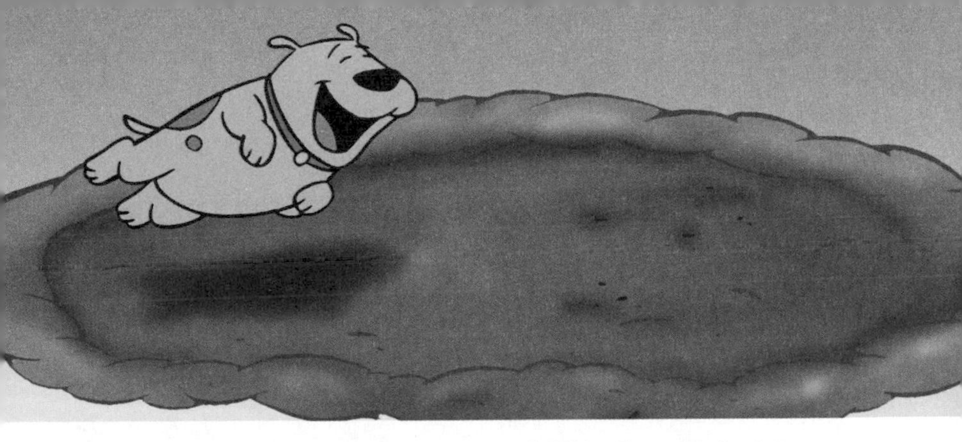

Clifford, Cleo, and K.C. quickly padded over. "Are you okay?" Clifford asked.

T-Bone shook off the dirt. "I guess so. But what happened to the merry-go-round?"

Everyone stared at the empty space.

"It's gone!" Clifford cried.

The Merry-go-round Is Missing

T-Bone's eyes opened wide. "The merry-go-round was here yesterday," he said.

"Somebody stole it!" Cleo cried.

"We don't know that, Cleo," Clifford told his friend. He didn't want to think there was a thief on Birdwell Island. "We just know it's missing."

"Wow!" K.C. grinned. "We've got a real mystery here. I bet Detective Mike could figure it out."

“Who’s Detective Mike?” asked Cleo.

“Come on,” said K.C. “I’ll show you.”

Everyone followed K.C. back home. Mrs. Young was sleeping. So

K.C. carried the book bag outside. Then he nosed out the Detective Mike book.

All the dogs crowded around. "Detective Mike can solve any

mystery in the world!" K.C. pointed to a picture. "That's him!"

"Wow," said Clifford. "Do you think he could figure out our mystery?"

K.C. thought a moment. "Well . . . he's not real . . . but maybe his book could teach *us* what to do."

"Let's see." K.C. flipped through some pages. "What does Detective Mike do first? How does he find clues?"

K.C. stopped at a page near the beginning. He looked at it carefully. "Detective Mike has a stakeout."

T-Bone jumped for joy. "Steak out? *Mmmm-mmm*. Steak! I love steak!"

Clifford smacked his lips. "Me, too!"

"Me, three!" Cleo shouted. "Let's have a steak out!"

K.C. clapped his paws for quiet. "Hold it, everyone!"

T-Bone stopped jumping. Cleo stopped shouting. And Clifford stopped smacking. "What?" they all asked.

"A stakeout doesn't mean you eat steak."

"Oh!" T-Bone's ears drooped.

There was nothing he liked better than a good meal.

K.C. pointed to the page. "A stakeout means you hide near the scene of the mystery. Then you see who shows up!"

"But what if no one shows up?" Clifford felt confused. "Then what do you eat?"

"I think we better pack a lunch," said Cleo.

T-Bone nodded. "With lots of Tummy Yummies!"

“I like Bowser Bites,” Clifford added. “Especially the barbecue-flavored ones —”

“Guys!” K.C. interrupted. “Forget the food. It’s not important.”

“It’s not?” said T-Bone.

“No. The important thing is to be there. In case someone shows up.” K.C. put the book into the book bag. Then he slung it over his neck. “To the playground!”

Dog Detectives

"First things first," K.C. decided when they got to the playground. "We have to find hiding spots for the stakeout."

"Okay, Detective Cleo," he said. "You hide in the slide. Inside the tunnel at the top. I'll be in the bushes. And Detective Clifford?"

"Here I am!" Clifford's head popped over the handball court wall.

K.C. smiled. “You found a great place!” He looked around. “Now where’s Detective T-Bone?”

Cleo pointed her paw. “Here he comes!”

Slowly, T-Bone walked toward them. He was dragging a big bag. “Snacks!” he explained. “Since we don’t have any steak!”

Squeak. Squeak.

The dogs perked up their ears. *Squeak! Squeak!* Someone was coming.

"Sounds like a wagon, too!" K.C. whispered. "Hide!"

K.C. ran to the bushes. Clifford ducked behind the wall. Cleo snuck into the slide tunnel.

T-Bone looked around. Where should he hide? He had it! In the snack bag. Quickly, he jumped inside.

Squeak. Squeak. The wagon was coming closer.

Clifford peeked out from his hiding spot. "It's Charley!" he said softly.

Charley was Emily Elizabeth's friend. Clifford liked him, too. But why was he pulling a wagon to the playground? And why did the wagon have a big crate on it?

He couldn't have anything to do with the missing merry-go-round!

Could he?

“Wow,” said Charley. He stopped where the merry-go-round used to be. “They took it already.” He stood there a moment longer. Then he turned to leave.

Cleo slipped down the slide a bit. She wanted to see where Charley was going. She watched him walk out of the playground . . . turn left . . .

She slid down a little more. He was going —

“Oops!” Cleo tumbled to the ground.

She jumped up and ran to the others.

"Did you hear that?" she asked, excited. "Charley knows something. He said, 'They took it already.' He knows who *they* are!"

"I didn't hear anything," K.C. said. "Did you, Clifford?"

"No. I was too far away. How about you, T-Bone?"

Munch, munch. T-Bone swallowed. Then he said, "Sorry. I only heard chewing sounds."

Cleo tossed her head. "Well, I heard him!"

“We believe you, Cleo,” Clifford said. “We just don’t know what to do about it.”

K.C. opened the Detective Mike book. “Let’s see what Mike would do!”

Tailing Charley

Everyone looked at the Detective Mike picture. "It looks like Mike is following that guy," said T-Bone.

K.C. nodded. "He's tailing him."

T-Bone wagged his tail. "I've got a tail!"

"Me, too!" said Cleo.

"Me, too!" Clifford added.

"Not that kind of tail," K.C. explained. "Tailing means you

follow someone. And they don't see you!"

Clifford and T-Bone felt a little disappointed. Tailing didn't have anything to do with having a tail. But Cleo was determined. She wanted to do this detective stuff. And she wanted to do it right. "Well, great! Let's tail Charley!"

She started out of the playground. K.C. and Clifford followed right behind. T-Bone trailed a bit. Then he stopped. He gazed back at his snack bag.

"Uh, I think I should stay here. You know, do more stakeout. Just in case."

Clifford, Cleo, and K.C. tailed Charley into town. They didn't want Charley to see them. So they stayed far behind.

Charley walked up one street, then down another. Finally, he stopped in front of a store.

Cleo pointed across the street. "It's the Seashell Shop!"

Charley parked his wagon by the entrance. Then he walked inside.

K.C. nodded. "Okay, he can't

see us now. Detective Mike would use this time to investigate."

"What's *investigate*?" Cleo said.

"It means you look at things very closely. So, Cleo, go look closely at Charley's crate."

"Right!" said Cleo. She tiptoed across the street. Good. It was all clear. Charley was nowhere in sight. She stuck her head inside the crate.

"Ouch, ouch, ouch!"

Crabs sprang up and gripped her fur.

"Ouch is right," said Clifford. He started across the street to help.

But just then Charley came out. "A little curious, Cleo?" One by one, Charley pulled off the crabs. "Back in the crate you go!" he said.

Charley patted Cleo, making sure she was okay. "I have to take the crabs to my dad's restaurant," he explained. "See you later."

Once Charley had gone, K.C. and Clifford padded over.

"I don't think those crabs took the merry-go-round," Clifford said. "And I don't think Charley did, either."

Cleo and Clifford looked at K.C. "What's next?" asked Clifford.

"Back to the park!" K.C. decided. "Let's see how Detective T-Bone is doing with his stakeout!"

Detective Mike Helps Again

A few minutes later, the dogs were back at the park.

"Oh, no!" cried Cleo.

Clifford gazed at another empty spot in the playground. "The swings are missing now!"

"Good thing Detective T-Bone

was here," K.C. said. "He can tell us what happened."

Cleo shook her head. "I don't think so."

She pointed to T-Bone. He was fast asleep, inside his empty snack bag.

Cleo stepped over. "T-Bone!" she shouted. "We're back!"

"Huh?" T-Bone opened one eye, then the other. "What?"

Clifford knelt closer. "Did you see anything, T-Bone?"

T-Bone rubbed his eyes. He looked around. "Hey! What happened to the swings?"

"I guess he didn't see anything," Cleo said.

But Clifford didn't want to give up. "Did you see anything at all, T?"

T-Bone looked up at his friend. He felt terrible. "I — I — I don't think so. I'm sorry."

"Don't worry." K.C. flipped open the Detective Mike book. "We've got Detective Mike to help us, too."

Inside, K.C. found another picture. Detective Mike was sitting in a restaurant. He was tilting his head toward other tables.

"He's listening to people talk," said Clifford.

"He's getting information," K.C. agreed.

"He's snooping!" Cleo added.

"And sniffing!" T-Bone said, eyeing the food in the picture.

"I know," said Clifford. "We can get lunch at my house, and see if anyone is around, talking!"

"Lunch!" said T-Bone happily.

Cleo nodded. "All this detective work is making me hungry."

"Let's go to Clifford's house!" said K.C.

Snooping and Sniffing

Emily Elizabeth was happy to give the dogs lunch. She led everyone to the backyard.

"Here you go," she said. She poured one bowl for Cleo, one for T-Bone, and one for K.C. She fed Clifford last — putting his food

into a dog dish as big as a giant bathtub.

Everyone munched on the food.

"This is great." T-Bone slurped. "But no one is here. And Emily Elizabeth isn't talking at all!"

Just then Jetta poked her head around the yard. "Hi!" she called out.

"Shh!" whispered Clifford. "Pretend to eat!" He lifted an ear to listen.

"Who needs to pretend!" said T-Bone.

"How are you, Jetta?" asked Emily Elizabeth.

"Great!" Jetta tossed her ponytail. "Do you want to come over to my house?" she asked Emily Elizabeth. "I've got something to show you."

"What is it?" Emily Elizabeth asked.

Jetta hopped up and down, excited. "It's a swing set!"

The dogs stopped eating — even T-Bone.

"She has the swings! She must have taken the merry-go-round, too," whispered K.C. "Let's go to her house."

In a flash, the dogs raced off.

"Wait, Clifford," Emily Elizabeth called. "You didn't finish your lunch!"

Swing Surprise

In minutes, the dog detectives stood in front of Jetta's home. Her dog, Mac, sat on the steps. He was chewing a bone.

Could Mac be in on it? Clifford wondered.

"Act like we're here to visit," said K.C. "Nothing else."

"Hi, Mac," said Clifford. "What are you doing?"

Mac shrugged. "What does it look like I'm doing?"

"Chewing a bone?" said T-Bone, trying to be helpful.

"Good detective work, T," Cleo whispered.

Mac stood up. "Right. Now I'm going to bury it."

He walked around the house to the back. The other dogs followed.

"We'll help!" said Clifford.

"That's okay, I know just the spot where I'm going to dig," said Mac. Still, everyone stayed close behind.

Squeak! Squeak!

"Sounds like a swing," said Clifford.

"This is it!" K.C. said happily. "We're going to find the swings and merry-go-round right here!"

They turned the corner. And there was a swing set.

But it was a brand-new swing set! Not the old, rusty one from the playground. And there wasn't a merry-go-round in sight.

"Oh." Clifford stopped short.

K.C. sighed. All that snooping for nothing. Then he remembered what Detective Mike once said: "Sometimes you have to start at the beginning, all over again."

"Back to the playground!" K.C. told his friends.

What's Missing Now?

Cleo, T-Bone, and K.C. climbed onto Clifford's back. He gave them a ride to the playground.

All of a sudden, he stopped short. The other dogs tumbled off.

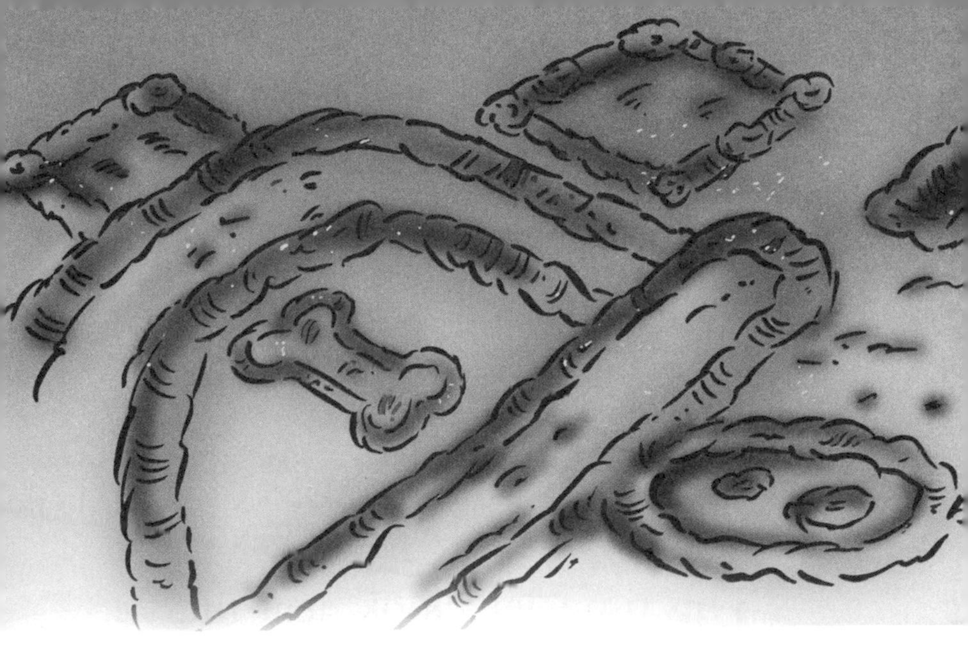

"I can't believe it!" said Clifford, surprised.

"Can't believe what?" Cleo scrambled to her feet.

"Look!"

The dogs gazed around the playground. "Now everything is missing!" T-Bone gasped.

The seesaw, the monkey bars, and the slide were gone, too. Everything had disappeared.

Cleo sighed. "Does Detective Mike say anything else?" she asked K.C.

"This time, let's look near the end." K.C. opened the book.

In one picture, Mike held a magnifying glass.

"He had that in another picture, too," said Clifford. "But we don't have one."

“Look what he’s doing!” cried K.C. “He’s searching for clues. And see what he’s looking at!”

Cleo peered at the page. “Tire tracks?”

“Right. And we have those!” K.C. pointed to a set of tracks. They circled all around the playground. “Maybe they’ll lead us to something.”

“What are we waiting for?” said Cleo. “Let’s follow them!”

Follow Those Tracks!

Noses to the ground, the dogs sniffed the tracks. They followed them out of the park . . . down some streets . . . and, finally, to the Birdwell Island docks.

"Looks like the tracks stop here!" said K.C.

Cleo pointed to a truck. "That pickup truck made the tracks!"

"And it's in front of a warehouse," Clifford said. "A place

to store big things! Like playground equipment!"

T-Bone squinted at the truck. "Hey!" he said to K.C. "Doesn't that belong to Bruno?"

K.C. lived with Mrs. Young — and her son, Bruno. Bruno was a housepainter. And his truck had a big paintbrush on its side.

K.C. looked closer. "It *is* Bruno's truck!"

The warehouse door swung open.

"Quick! Hide!" said K.C.

The dogs scrambled to the side of the building.

Bruno walked outside. Then he pulled out the seesaw from his truck. Grunting, he carried it inside.

K.C.'s eyes opened wide. "What is Bruno doing?"

Then Clifford spied someone else. "Look!"

"Oh, my!" T-Bone gasped. "Sheriff Lewis!"

Clifford couldn't believe it. T-Bone's owner! Here, at a scene of the crime. He was smiling and talking to Bruno.

Did they both take the playground equipment?

Cleo's Idea

K.C. felt terrible. "I can't believe Bruno would take the equipment."

"Or Sheriff Lewis!" T-Bone added.

Quickly, K.C. grabbed the detective book. "There's got to be more to this. What would Detective Mike do now?"

He flipped through page after page. "Nothing," he muttered. "Nothing. Nothing. Hey!" He stopped. "Check this out!"

In the picture, Mike held a glass up to his ear. He was pressing it against a wall.

Clifford took a closer look. "He's using that glass to listen. People are talking on the other side of the wall. And he wants to hear them."

K.C. snuck a peek at Bruno and Sheriff Lewis. They were moving around the truck, talking. "We need to hear what they are saying. But we don't have a glass!"

Cleo jumped like she had fleas. "I know what we can do!"

She raced to a garden hose lying on the ground. She grabbed one end in her mouth. Then she crawled on her stomach . . . under the truck . . . closer to Sheriff Lewis and Bruno . . . closer . . . closer.

Plop! She dropped the hose by their feet. Then she slunk away.

The dogs gathered around the other end of the hose.

They could hear voices. "It works!" said Clifford. They bent closer to listen.

"The kids are going to love this," Bruno told Sheriff Lewis. "I will paint the old playground equipment in bright new colors."

"We can take it all back tomorrow," said Sheriff Lewis.

T-Bone grinned. "Did you hear that? Bruno is painting the equipment!"

"And Sheriff Lewis is helping!" Cleo said.

Clifford nodded and smiled. "So that's what's going on." He didn't think anyone would steal the equipment. And he was right!

Everyone was happy. Except for K.C. He wasn't saying a word.

Mystery Solved!

"What's the matter, K.C.?" asked T-Bone.

"I was hoping we would solve a real mystery," said K.C.

Clifford swung his head close to his friend. "But we did, K.C. — even if there aren't any bad guys. And remember, we all worked together. First we did the stakeout. Then we tailed Charley."

"And don't forget snooping!" Cleo put in.

"Right," Clifford agreed. "And finally, we found out what happened to the missing stuff!"

K.C. wagged his tail. "Wow! You're right, Clifford. We did solve a mystery. Just like Detective Mike. *The Mystery of the Missing Merry-go-round*!"

Later, Mrs. Young read K.C. a new Detective Mike book.

“It’s *The Mystery of the Missing Elephant*,” she said.

Clifford, Cleo, and T-Bone edged closer. This time, they were listening, too!